Imara has lived a life separate from her family. She wasn't shunned, just never acknowledged. The seventh child of a seventh child, she had had the bad taste to be born a girl. Her father's family had no use for a girl, so she was sent to a city where the populace didn't use magic.

Now that she is grown and entering college, she has chosen the best magical college in the country. It just happens to be located in her birth city.

When family begins to encroach on her education and someone threatens her life, can her new familiar do as he promised and keep her safe, or will Imara have to use what little magic she has learned to keep herself alive? Either way, things are going to be unpleasant.

Soul Casting 101
The Hellkitten Chronicles
Book One

By

Viola Grace

Mirrin was exhausted but delighted. She had carried out her contract and given her husband what he wanted and a little more.

The nurse turned toward him, holding the dual burdens. "Mr. Demiel, here are your children."

Mirrin watched as her husband started forward and then paused. He growled, "Which one is my son?"

The nurse frowned. "Um, here. This is your son."

Mirrin reached out for her daughter. "Please give her to me."

Holding his precious son in his awkward arms, he shook his head. "Mirrin, you know we are not going to keep her. I have what the family needed. We have the seventh son of the seventh son. The lucky one. Our fortunes are going to turn, but in the meantime, we are not going to feed an extra mouth. You know that arrangements have been made."

"Desmond! It is just a little girl. What kind of harm could she do?"

The nurse was hesitating with the little girl in her arms.

Mirrin pushed herself up, her body protesting mightily. "Give her to me. She may leave tomorrow, but today, she is my baby. My little Imara."

"Mirrin, let her go. She is unlucky."

"You have your seventh son, Desmond. Our contract is over. I am taking our daughter to Sakenta, and then, I am leaving."

Her husband was shocked. "What? You have seven sons to care for."

"My contract was to bear you your

seventh son. I did that. I am not going to live with you screaming and ordering me around anymore. You wanted those hellions, you deal with them. I have my own life that I want to get back to." Mirrin was somber as she stroked the pink cheek of her daughter.

She couldn't keep her girl. All children that she bore were the sole responsibility of the Demiel family. She was simply a conduit of her family's genes and their own debt to the Demiels. If she could keep her daughter, she would, but that wasn't in her contract.

Imara Demiel was going to grow up without the burden of a family history or being a ley-line mage. Her world was going to be wide open, and Mirrin hoped she lived long enough to see it.

Against all odds, Imara had been born before her brother in the same minute. She was the seventh child of a seventh child, and while the Demiel's didn't set any store by that, Mirrin knew that her family would cherish their new addition if they were allowed to claim her. The Deepford-Smythe family would keep an eye out for their newest member. They may have lost everything, including their family honour, but they loved their own.

Little Imara couldn't have direct contact with her mother, but the Deepford-Smythe family would find her and take care of her. Some way, some how, her daughter would know how much she was wanted.

The hospital was silent as Mirrin walked slowly to the nursery. She just wanted to hold her daughter one more time before she was taken.

Mirrin crept into the nursery, reading the names on the plastic cribs until she found the one that said Demiel. The blue wrappings adorned her son, so she stepped to the next crib only to find it empty. There was no tag, no baby.

"They took her away at dinner. Your people said they will care for her." A nurse stood there with a sad but kind expression on her face.

Mirrin dropped to her knees. "Gone?"

The woman came over and placed her hand on Mirrin's shoulder. "Yes, Mrs. Demiel. Your daughter is gone; now, let's get you back to bed."

She got to her feet, and as they left the nursery, Mirrin kept looking back at the empty crib that should have contained a baby she should have been able to keep. Too many *shoulds*.

Mirrin hoped her daughter got the freedom and power that she had been born to wield, and she wished more than anything that her father never found out what she was.

The seventh child of the seventh child was just as powerful as a seventh son.

With Mirrin and Desmond both seventh children, their seventh child was bound to be immensely powerful. Their seventh child was their daughter, and Desmond would never know.

Chapter One

"Imra, we need a calm-down at twelve B. There is a wild mix of something going on."

Imara looked at him with a weary gaze. "Come on, it's my last night."

"This is your job, Imra. Your last night to do it."

She made a face at Death Keeper Thomins and got to her feet. Most of the students in her high school were not fortunate enough to find a job at the repository of the dead. Being an Apprentice Death Keeper had let her save up, and when she was ready to apply, she had gotten into the most prestigious magic college for three provinces.

The next day she left for her new school to learn the basics of charms, spells and magic in general. For that night, she had to find out what was going on in twelve B.

She smoothed her cassock and lit the lantern outside the door. With a sense of finality, Imara hooked it onto her staff and walked through the repository, past the active graves until she reached what was supposed to be the newly silent.

Imara walked down the rows of those who had been retired by their families, their knowledge no longer required.

Her lantern illuminated the three specters floating above their resting places. "Good evening, lady and gentlemen. Is there any particular reason for your rising?"

She approached them and set the lantern on the grass. She folded her hands in front of her and waited.

Madame Gregoria Limack floated toward her and extended her hand. Imara mimicked her gesture and smiled as the specter made contact.

We worked out that you are leaving us. We wished to give you a proper send off. You have been a treasure to watch as you grew into the young lady before us.

"Thank you. I will be sorry to leave, but I am very excited to go to Depford College."

One of the men floated forward and touched her arm. *We are excited for you, as much as we are able. We wish you luck, and we wanted to offer you a gift.*

She blinked at Mr. Frimaldi. "Thank you for the thought."

Mr. Exeter grinned and touched her shoulder. *We managed to arrange it with a little help.*

"Well, Imra, you seem to have made an impression on our guests."

She turned to see Thomins approaching. He was grinning, and he had a small object in the hand not holding the lantern.

"You are in on this?"

"They asked me when we were moving them. They wanted to give you something and forced their families to chip in. It was hilarious." As a Death Keeper, he always sided with the guests. They were the ones he had to work with, after all.

She stared at the spectral and physical gathering around her. "You threatened your families?"

Madame Leemra laughed silently. *We did not give them all our secrets. They may have decided to retire us, but that does not mean we have been drained of all knowledge. We are not leaving until we are good and ready.*

Imara sighed. "You didn't have to do anything."

Thomins smirked. "They wanted to. This is a letter to the Dean of the College. There is also a small box with a letter in it. They are yours with the compliments and best wishes from our locals."

She took the gifts and looked and them with stunned amazement. "Thank you. Thank you all so much."

They converged on her and caressed her cheeks and arms. She caught the thoughts, the well wishes and the flashes of them sending their children and grandchildren off to college. She was their chance to live a little past the veil of death.

Silently, she promised to check in with them whenever possible. They laughed at that. She was going to be getting on with her life and that was good. Life was for living, and for *the* living. They were just happy that they could force their descendants to contribute to their going-away gift.

The party lasted for an hour, and then, the inhabitants of twelve B retired for the evening, their energy spent. The copies of ancient mages retreated to their soul stones and rested in the monuments that held them. A living life was reduced to a six-inch wide by three-foot high pillar of stone with the gem embedded in it.

As an Apprentice Death Keeper, she had had to monitor the energy level in the stones and keep them clean. Planting flowers around them that bloomed and glowed in the darkness was something she did on her breaks. Apparently, it was appreciated.

She wished she could do more for them than tend their tombs, but that was the job, so she did it.

When they all winked out, she picked up her staff and lantern, holding the gift with the other hand.

Thomins was grinning at her. "There were others who made their families contribute, but they have faded already."

"Why?" They returned to the office next to the parking lot.

"Because for a moment when they met you, they saw someone with potential for a future that they wanted to contribute to. They do not get many opportunities to participate in the living world."

Imara nodded. "I know that, but why me?"

"Madame Ikohn is one of your ancestors. She needled the others into participating since she could not address you directly." Thomins dropped that little bombshell casually.

"My... I did not think I had family here."

He chuckled. "She was born here and moved when she married. She was a contract bride and returned to her family when the contract was fulfilled. I believe she was deputy mayor for a decade."

Imara's mind was spinning as they extinguished and stowed the lanterns. She set the staff in its slot and looked at the objects in her hand. The letter addressed to the Dean of Students was a heavy, cream-coloured parchment with a black wax seal. She didn't recognise the family mark, but she would deliver the letter.

The box that was only slightly larger than the letter and was black and purple, carved with glyphs and humming with power.

"I don't think I can accept this. It looks old."

Thomins grinned and sat with his feet up on his desk. "They ordered the family to give it to you, so it is yours. I have a record of transfer if anyone requires it."

"Which family is it from?"

He chuckled. "You will have to open it and see, but it is the end of your shift and you need to be getting that transport to the college."

"I am driving. It is only two hours away."

"Then, you had better be going. It has been fun having you here, but your destiny lies with the living. I have been around long enough to know that. Life as a Death Keeper is not for you."

She walked over and extended her hand. "Thanks for all that you have shown me, Thomins. You truly have a knack for soul manipulation that is enviable."

He gripped her hand and grinned. "You were definitely grasping the basics. I have high hopes for your future studies. Don't be a stranger."

Imara nodded and swallowed the lump in her throat. "Thanks. I will keep you posted on my progress."

"Do, or I will call the school myself. I am fairly sure that I am going to be inundated with status requests from the occupants here. I am going to need every tidbit of your life that you can share."

She laughed. "They are relentless."

"They are, but stimulation is good for them. It makes them last longer."

She looked through the window at the carefully organized repository of mind imprints held together inside painstakingly enchanted gemstones. The soul might be gone but the mind remained, and the minds needed stimulation. She had unwittingly provided that stimulation with her tales of high school and her boarding house.

Her life had become their link to the living world. She was going to miss being that bridge.

She sniffled as she drove from the boarding house to her new—

temporary—home at the college. The box was on the passenger seat next to her, along with the letter.

Her bags were in the back seat. A few weeks of clothing, notebooks and pens were all that she owned.

Dawn was a thing of the past, and she would be reaching the college in minutes. A nervous clenching of her stomach reminded her that she hadn't had breakfast, or dinner for that matter.

Her first stop was the office of the dean of students, and after that, she was heading straight to registration.

Chapter Two

The parking spot she had been as-signed was at the far end of the universe from any of the class buildings. It wasn't great, but it was secure.

Imara tucked the letter into her jacket and zipped the box into her backpack. Her suitcase had excellent wheels, and it would make a lot of noise but remain intact wherever she dragged it. It was her big splurge purchase, aside from tuition and lodgings.

She locked her car, checked the map on her phone and went to deliver the letter.

Senior students and freshman were beginning to arrive on campus. She passed nearly a dozen as she hauled the rumbling case across the sidewalks and pathways.

The soil under her feet contained magic. The college had been built on a wave site, and the ancient magic still simmered below the surface. This was where she would learn to hone the skills she had been born with.

The feeling of walking through somewhere she had always been meant to be was strange. Sakenta had been a great place to grow up, but the lack of magic use in the population was a stark reminder that she didn't belong. Each and every day she was thankful for the guidance counsellor that had put her in touch with the Death Keepers. It was a small outlet, but it had been welcome. Her first experience with using magic had been talking to the dead. It was not a normal introduction, yet it had confirmed her desire to seek out more information and education on the subject. She was destined for magic.

Anticipation was pushing past her hunger. The dean of students was located in the same building as registration, which meant that there was only a small diversion necessary.

She crossed the inlaid marble floor, passed the registration tables for first years and walked up two flights of stairs to the dean's office.

Behind the heavy door, she found a young man seated behind a desk, and he appeared irritated as he set his phone down. "Can I help you?"

She reached into her jacket and pulled out the letter. "I have this for the Dean of Students."

The young man with the dark brown hair and deep green eyes smiled. "I will give it to him."

Her fingers tightened. "I think I am supposed to deliver it myself."

"You have brought it to his offices. That means you have delivered it. Give it to me, and I will send it through."

She didn't know what that meant, but she extended the heavy parchment to him.

Without looking at it, he opened a small, flat box on his desk and he set the letter inside. He closed the box while smirking at her, and the glyphs glowed. "There, the dean has it. You can be on your way."

She opened and closed her hands, turned and hauled her stuff out of the room, feeling as if something was undone.

Ah well, there was registration, checking into her room and getting a meal to do before she could spend some time focusing on what she had left undone.

The young man named Anton had

given her excellent directions on how to find Reegar Hall. The pity in his eyes was something she could have done without, but as long as the place had space for her to sleep and study, she had what she needed.

Going to magical college on a budget was not going to be easy.

Imara looked at the exterior of Reegar Hall, and she wrinkled her nose. Where the other buildings had ancient brick and stone, Reegar was all concrete and cracked mortar. She walked inside and was greeted by a chipper redhead who seemed relieved to have something to do.

"Hiya, are you lost?"

"No. I am one of the students assigned to Reegar."

"Oh. Oh!" The woman pumped her hand happily. "I am the Resident Advisor for Reegar Hall. My name is Bara. Bara Wilmington."

"Imara Mirrin. First year."

"Right, of course. Do you have your food card?"

"I do. It is in my pack."

"Well, get it out and I will seal it to you. It is best to do it right away. Folks tend to lose them, and it costs a fortune to replace them."

Imara fished around in her welcome envelop and pulled out the two-by-one inch card. "Got it."

"Great. Give me your wrist." Bara plucked the card from her fingers and took her left wrist. With a bit of pressure and some muttered words, the card sealed itself to Imara's skin. It became as flexible as a tattoo but only visible when the light skimmed across it.

Bara smiled. "I specialise in bio-manipulation magic. If you take any shifter courses, let me know. Now, come this way. You are the only confirmed booking this year, so it will be just us in the entire hall."

"Why?"

"It isn't the most prestigious, and Magus Reegar was an insane genius who is said to haunt this hall."

Imara followed her own personal RA up the steps and down the hall to the rooms. "That is probably why they suggested it to me. I have met a specter or two in my life."

"Really? How many?"

"Two hundred and thirty-four, give or take." She hauled her bag along after her and looked at the plain, uninspired decoration. It was as if someone had forced the building to be bland.

Bara paused and looked back. "That is a weird coincidence."

"Not really. I knew about the haunting and the price was right. One was an enticement and the other wouldn't scare me off. Guess which was which." She grinned and hoisted her bag up next to her.

Bara waved her arms. "You have your pick of any of the rooms. It will key to you and your familiar when it arrives."

Imara paused. "My familiar?"

"Yes. Your registration indicated that you were taking the Soul Casting course. A familiar is a requirement." Bara frowned. "You do have one, don't you?"

Imara felt her heart sink. She had looked forward to taking that course. "No."

"I am sure you can work something out. The practical part of the course is a few weeks in." Bara reached out and patted her arm.

Imara looked down the hall and took a deep breath. She let her instinct be her guide, and she gripped her suitcase. With a slow exhalation, she sent the luggage down the halls on its wheels. It careened from side to side, twisting and rolling to a stop in front of the door on the left at the end of the hall.

Bara nodded approvingly. "That is a good choice. It has windows that open if you are doing any light spell work."

Imara walked to her new door and pressed her hand against the door handle. It fought her for a moment before it opened, and she looked at her new domain.

The luggage rolled inside as if it knew home when it saw it. Imara turned to Bara. "I suppose I am home."

Bara nodded. "Please. Settle in. I will be on the main floor if you want a tour."

Imara gave her a short smile. "I will be down in a few minutes. This won't take long."

The door swung closed in Bara's face. Apparently, the hall wanted her to settle in as well.

Imara looked around and sighed. The décor was bland, but it was neat and clean. The bed was a double, covered with white sheets, a polar fleece blanket and fluffed pillows.

The bookshelf was empty, and the desk was plain but pristine. The chair had four legs instead of rollers, and the floor was smooth cement.

She needed a small carpet. That much was certain.

Imara opened her luggage and put her books on the shelf. Her clothing was all foldable, and it slid into the dresser next to her closet without any trouble. There was plenty of room to hide a body in the empty drawers.

"Wow, this is better than I thought."

"Thank you, I do try, but I am restricted by the college from doing anything else." A man walked through her wall. His clothing gave no hint as to his date of death, but his vibe was definitely that of the dead.

She smiled tightly. "Magus Reegar, I presume?"

"Yes. You are the new student."

"I am. Imara Mirrin."

He extended his hand. "That is not your full name."

"No, but you can call me Imra." She placed her hand next to his and let him close the gap between them.

The peculiar cool touch of a ghost was augmented by the crackle of active magic. That wasn't right.

She flexed her fingers when he withdrew his hand. "You are not a standard ghost."

He grinned, his mustache turned up with his lips and the slicked-back hair gleamed in the light streaming in through the window. He almost appeared solid. There was only the hint of translucence through his grey wool suit.

"You are correct. I died in this building by another's hand."

"So, your power came with you."

He chuckled. "I knew you would be a

good fit here. You have the run of the building."

"Excellent. Please don't come in without knocking. I am a woman living alone, and I don't need to worry about warding myself from nocturnal specters."

"I was expecting a little more trepidation."

She chuckled. "It takes more than a magical man without a body to creep me out. I am here to learn and get an education that I can work with."

She watched his dark features as he eyed her up and down. She took in the clothing from another era that wasn't quite at odds with contemporary garb. He had been a sharp dresser, and even the creases in his trousers had made it into the afterlife.

"You are here because it is inexpensive, but I trusted my instincts when you applied for residency here. I did nothing to interfere with the application. They might have called me mad, but aside from one day where I didn't trust my own judgement and ended up haunting my own hall, I have always gone with my instincts. I will offer you what help I can, but you are right. You are here to study. I will respect that and make sure to knock. Welcome to Reegar Hall."

He disappeared as suddenly as he had appeared, leaving Imara alone in her room.

"That was interesting. He even had an audio presence. That was definitely different."

Talking to herself was par for the course. It didn't matter who was around, but there was usually something or someone listening.

Her stomach growled loudly, and she grinned. It was time to put it to rest.

Brunch was left on her agenda, and then, she was heading to the bookstore.

Half her books were online, but the other half were beginner enchantment books.

Coffee and books were in her future. That much was certain.

Chapter Three

ara was an excellent hostess, and she seemed exceptionally happy to have another body in the building.

"How many folks can fit in Reegar Hall?"

"Fifty. He only accepts the ones that he thinks will do credit to the hall."

Imara grinned. "Which is us."

"Precisely. Cappucino?"

"Three is usually my limit, but sure." Imara watched as her companion fired up the machine once again.

The outfitting of the study area was incredible. The true passion of Magus Reegar was displayed in the in-house library and snack bar.

The bagel had stopped the gnawing hunger; the fruit salad had given her a burst of energy. Now on her fourth coffee, she was going to be able to head straight to the bookstore to get the last of her supplies.

Bara sat across from her again. "So, what are you going to do about the familiar?"

"Can't I just get a pet?"

The coughing and spluttering that Bara engaged in was enough of an answer.

Imara sipped at her drink. "Not a good idea?"

"Not unless you want to explode a bunch before you find one that can hold all your power. That is what the familiars do. They act as a repository to keep your essentials safe while the rest of you is playing with spells."

Bara wrinkled her nose. "See the dean of students. He can look into your family lines to see if you have any familiars available."

Imara leaned forward. "Family lines?"

"Sure. At some point, most mage families have made familiars for their children. Or, they have had them made."

"Damn. Well, I guess I am going to have to drop a class before I even get started." Imara heaved a deep sigh. "That sucks."

"Seriously, check with the dean. He has all the records for each student." Bara bit into a muffin and looked up in surprise when a loud knock sounded. "Whaff vah hew?"

"Should I get it?"

The RA swallowed hard and shook her head. "Nope. This is why I get to live here and get a stipend. I will be right back."

Bara brushed her fingers on her jeans as she crossed the room and headed for the hallway leading to the front door.

The expression on her face could only

be called bemused when Bara returned with a blue-tinged man trailing after her.

"Uh, Imara, it is for you."

The man was carrying a briefcase, and he looked at her intently as he approached. "Miss Mirrin?"

She got to her feet to greet him. "Yes."

"I am Yringar Mornwalker, dean of students."

"Oh. That is funny. Bara was just saying that I should speak with you." She extended her hand.

The prickle of cold ran up her arm as he returned the greeting.

"Ms. Wilmington, may we have the room please? I have a great deal to discuss with Ms. Mirrin, and I believe discretion is paramount."

"Of course. I will wait outside the door in case Magus Reegar authorized anyone else this year and didn't mention it."

Bara smiled and flicked some of her red tresses over one shoulder. She headed for the hallway, and Imara was alone with a strange, blue man.

He smiled tightly and took the spot in the comfortable chair, swamping it with his size.

Imara couldn't help but stare. "You are... not human?"

He grinned. "I am supposing that you have not met many extra-naturals in your life. I am a mixed-heritage frost giant. Now, I am here to discuss your inheritance."

"My what?"

"Your mother's family has set aside some funds for you, as well as books and a familiar."

Imara blinked. "I couldn't be that lucky. What familiar?"

"It has been in the Deepford-Smythe family for generations. Twenty generations to be precise. To be honest, I was shocked when I received that letter this morning. It took some doing to find your pedigree, but now that we have it, you are going to reap the full benefit of your connections."

He popped the clasps on the briefcase and opened it, pulling out a sheaf of papers four inches thick and studded with file folders and tabs.

"First, as you are an *Unknown,* we will go over your family histories and attachments. When that has been settled, we will get into your inheritances. You have several that have been given to you based on your mother's side of the family. They didn't have much money, but they did have power. The histories are now yours to go over at your leisure. I am sorry I took so long, but there were a lot of documents to copy."

He handed her the first folder and smiled. "You know your status?"

Imara held the file that she had

dreamed of since she was a teen. "Yes. I know that I was the extra in a contract bond. My brothers remained with my father, but there was no need for a daughter. I was sent to Sakenta and raised by the state and a family trust. My situation was to remain unknown to family until I became an adult. I was also considered to be unlucky."

"Only by your father's family. In your mother's notes to you, you were the lucky one. You were born seventh as the child of two seventh children. You are exceptionally lucky."

He fished out a folded sheet of paper. "Here is your family tree. You will need it for genealogy courses."

Imara's mind was whirling as she got family histories, lists of local relatives and an appointment card to meet with the Master of Familiars on campus. He would set her up with a link to her family beast.

She was hungry again by the time he was finished, but getting her familiar now took precedence to her belly.

"There are a lot of masters on the campus."

He smiled brightly and chuffed a laugh. "There are. We can't have folks being taught by just anyone. Everyone working as an instructor here is a master in his or her field. Thamus is the Master of Familiars. He teaches the higher levels how to create their own familiars. He also manages the inherited-familiar program."

"Right. Where do I go for that?"

"I will take you there. I believe you have enough to absorb for one day." He nodded. "Keep the appointment card to present to Thamus. He is a stickler for formalities."

She looked at the mountain of documents. "May I take this too my room before we go?"

"Certainly, but you do not need to remain here. There is a stipend allocated for your residence here at the college. It will fit you into a more... suitable location."

Imara looked around. "I like it here. It suits me. As long as my familiar is content with the space, I won't have anything to complain about."

"Are you sure?"

Magus Reegar floated into the room. "She said it suits her, Yringar. Leave her be."

The dean tensed. "I didn't know you were strong enough to skulk around here, Reegar."

Magus Reegar was nearly opaque as he approached them. "Ms. Mirrin gives off all kinds of energy. Forming something visible is child's play in comparison to what I am now capable of, just with a few hours of her under my roof."

The dean looked ill. "You are feeding

from her?"

Imara held up a hand to forestall the conversation. "I give off waves that are useful for the disembodied. I am looking forward to learning shielding techniques. I can still power Reegar if he asks after I can put a cork in the fountain, but until then, he can hold conversations like a normal person and even read a book if he so chooses."

She got to her feet with her armloads of paperwork. "I will be right back."

Her desk received the paperwork without even shuddering, which was a miracle given how flimsy it had seemed on first inspection.

She clutched the card with the details of her familiar assignment and returned to the lounge.

Reegar was in the stacks of books and looking for his favourites.

She smiled at the giant who was waiting for her. "I am ready to go now."

"Good. I will take the time on the journey to ask you about your family name and why you don't use it."

She smirked. "Good luck with that."

They walked out of Reegar Hall, side by side. The walks were filling with new students and returning seniors. Whatever the other pedestrians were, they gave the dean a wide berth.

"Sir, if I may ask, why are you working at the human magic college?"

He smiled. "My people skills."

"I am guessing you don't have to use them often."

"No, but they are available when the need arises."

She grinned. They passed the main administration building and turned down toward a path leading to large, wide structures and open fields.

"So, Ms. Mirrin, why don't you use your family name?"

"Ah, well, that is just because my

mother's family name gave me too much trouble when I was young and my father's family didn't want me. I chose my mother's first name as my last because it seemed that she was the first person in my life who wanted anything to do with me. She made sure that I was given to a good institution in Sakenta, and they raised me with an eye to my future. Unfortunately, my family name made them treat me with odd attention. The Smythe name was on the front of the boarding school and nursery after all."

"So, when did you change it?"

"When I was changing from junior high to high school. I changed my name and had them set me in as a new student from out of the city. I changed boarding homes as well and started over."

"They allowed this?"

"Of course. I was an excellent student and a credit to the contract breeding that the Deepford-Smythes engage in.

They want me to be successful, so they are paying the bills for the most part."

He nodded. "I read that in the letter. Your Great Aunt is very proud of the work you have done to send yourself to college, but she has decided it is time for the family to truly step in."

"I was given to believe they were broke."

"They are, but there are family discounts to be had. There was a trust for you that wasn't activated because of the name change. That is being rectified as we speak."

"Excellent. More money means more courses."

"Oh, your courses are all complements of the college. The Depford of Depford College is one of your ancestors on your mother's side." He shrugged slightly. "It is all in the files."

She rubbed her forehead. "This is all a little much."

"Don't worry. Your familiar will be able to relieve some of that pressure." He chuckled. "Here we are."

They paused in front of a large blue barn painted with containment glyphs on every eave and every peak. It did, indeed, look like the right place. Whatever was conjured in that building would stay there unless it was deliberately set free.

She clutched the card with her familiar information and stepped up to the wide, black, double doors.

"Here is where I leave you. Simply hand the card to the first mage who asks you your business. They will handle it from there."

Without another word, the dean of students turned on his heel and left her at the base of the steps. It didn't fill her with enthusiasm for what came next, but if she had to, she had to.

Chapter Four

Standing in the foyer, she could see hundreds of containment glyphs covering the walls. They were slightly different from the ones used at the repository for the dead, but the theme was the same. Nothing gets out.

A young woman with glasses that had slid to the tip of her nose looked up with a smile. "May I help you?"

The ferret on the young woman's shoulder sat up on his hind legs in joint inquiry.

Imara extended her hand and gave the woman the card.

After a short glance at the card, the woman jumped to her feet and bobbed a short bow. "Please excuse me."

Imara looked at the portraits of mages and their familiars. Fierce mages were accompanied by fiercer beasts. It looked a little overwhelming to her, and she was about to skip the entire process when a voice called out to her.

"Imara Mirrin?"

She turned and blinked in surprise at the only figure that had appeared on campus wearing mages robes. "I am."

"I am Master Thamus. So, Yringar ran off? Typical. He will never live down the time he was working with the shifting class and got stuck in the body of a wolf. We had to house him here for weeks before the Shift Master came back from his sabbatical." He came forward and extended his hand to her.

She took in his healthy, tanned good looks, dark hair and rich pumpkin-coloured eyes. He was the epitome of magical health, and the embroidered robes that he wore added to the aura he presented.

Imara extended her hand and felt the power in his grip. "Pleased to meet you." She ignored the rest of the statement. It didn't pertain to her anyway.

"So, you are here to get your familiar?"

"Apparently." She gently tugged her hand free of his.

"Please, come this way. I will explain to you how this is going to work and what your familiar actually is."

"I would be delighted to learn."

He reached for her hand, but when she didn't extend it, he nodded and led the way.

They passed a wall of aquariums, a hall led to the sound of screeching birds; she could hear and smell animals all around her. It was an assault to the senses.

Thamus led her in what seemed like a

huge circle, but he finally turned down a hall that ended in a quiet room.

A gateway made of wood took up one wall. There were cushions in the center of a power circle and a low table waiting for them.

"Please have a seat. Are you comfortable with your grasp of what a familiar is?"

"Not particularly. It wasn't taught in Sakenta. We knew about the wave, but nothing more of magic was taught than that."

Master Thamus settled his robes around him in a dramatic and well-rehearsed fashion. "Well, in that case, I will give you the broad strokes for the type of familiar you are about to receive."

She nodded, and he waved his hand. A teapot lifted into the air from a sideboard and floated toward them. A stream of water was pulled out of a pitcher, and it cascaded in a column to meet the pot. Leaves from another container tumbled along.

It was a charming show, but she wished that Thamus could talk at the same time.

When he was using magic to heat the pot, he finally spoke. "While most mages take on a familiar as they advance in their careers, some inherit their familiars. These beasts are actually thinking magic users, bound in an animal form."

The pot lifted and tipped, filling two small cups.

"That doesn't sound pleasant for them."

"It isn't, but it is their fate. Families bound together. Hellhounds and mages linked by blood and power around the world."

"Hellhounds are people?"

"Mages who draw power from the demon zone."

She was nervous. "Is that why I am here?"

Thamus shook his head and sipped his tea. "No, your family is linked to a penal familiar."

"A what?"

"Your family and others were victims of an ancient mage. He killed several elders, and when he was caught,, he was put into service as a familiar for the eldest member of each family without a familiar, in rotation. The previous mage who had this familiar just passed last month. He is now up for claiming."

"I won him?"

He chuckled. "If you like to think of it that way. He can be an incredible assistant or an unbelievable burden. The choice is yours."

"What is his shifted form?"

Thamus smiled. "That is up to you. At the moment that the gateway opens, it will touch your mind and find the kind of beast you want your familiar to be. He will become that."

"So, he has no choice. If I want a goldfish, he becomes a goldfish."

"Not very useful, but yes. Think of what you want as companion, study guide and assistant, even mentor. That will be the form he takes. Now, drink your tea. It will help the gate reach your thoughts."

She reached out and picked up the cup. It tasted like drunk marshmallows. She finished it but wasn't happy about it.

Imara set the cup down with a click. "Done."

The pot filled it.

"Good. Do it again."

"What?"

"When your mind is ready, the portal will open. Until then, keep drinking the tea."

She made a face. "Why couldn't it have been coffee?"

"Because you can't hide herbs in coffee." He smiled politely. "Everyone expects herbal tea to taste peculiar."

She lifted the cup to her lips and slammed it back before setting it down. "How do I take care of it?"

"Well, his animal instinct will be strong, but when you need it, his human mind will spring to the foreground. He can eat what you eat, but figuring out the cleanliness routine will depend on what animal you choose."

She had been to one shot party before going to college, and the tea turned into an endless line of shots. Suddenly, the fish made sense. If she kept this up, her back teeth would be swimming.

"Tell me about yourself. What was your school like? What about your home?"

"Is this necessary?"

"You need to think of the moments when you felt you needed a champion.

Those are usually the places where the need is formed." Thamus smiled gently. "That is what the gateway is looking for so it can shape your familiar into something you truly want."

The light crackling of energy touched her thoughts.

"Whoa. I think something is happening."

"Keep drinking and talk to me about the worst moment in your life."

She felt the world fuzzing away at the edges, and she started to speak. "I had changed schools and was having my first day as the new me. No friends, no one I knew, and a new part of town. The new boarding house was austere and there was nothing living near it. The entire aura around my new neighborhood was static. Nothing grew. I wanted something of my own that had the potential to become something amazing. I wanted something I could touch and cuddle when I needed it. Something small, something cute. Something forever."

With every word, the prickling in her mind grew more intense, and as she finished her sentence and looked at the portal, fire blazed.

"Your familiar is about to arrive. Please extend your hand."

Imara kept her gaze on the portal and extended her hand. She felt a small burst of pain and heard chanting. Her focus was on the shadow forming in the swirling flames.

The vortex widened and the shadow grew larger. Imara pulled her hand away from Thamus and extended it toward the approaching figure.

Tears pricked her eyes as the creature came into focus. He was exactly what she wished for.

Trapped in his crystal cell, he flexed his fingers as he waited for the call. He was nearing the end of his sentence. Once he was free, he would be able to choose a dignified death or a new life under the aegis of the Mage Guild.

The families that he had harmed had been paid in labour, protection and guidance. Nearly a thousand years of servitude had been enough for him to consider his options and the evolution of magic.

The Mage Guild had come to his conclusion that magic obtained from the demon zone was not healthy for those around the mage using it. They had placed locks on everything related to demons, and now, he was in a world where his fondest dream had come true. He wished he could have been born a few centuries later.

The pull of magic came just in time.

He had been getting bored and nothing good came of getting bored.

The crystal opened, and he stepped free, heading for the platform where he would become the beast that his mage wanted. He had been wolves, lions, a unicorn, and even a small dragon. He wondered what magnificent incarnation he would take on next.

With a deep breath that took in no air, he walked forward and let the magic shape him to his new mage's will.

"Mew." The tiny black kitten made the small sound, and then, it blinked in surprise at its own voice.

"Mew. Mewmewmewmew."

She smiled and extended her hand, noting the blood on her fingers. He lifted his tiny head up and licked at the crimson drops.

Thamus's voice was strangled, but he stated. "And bound by blood, he shall serve you until the end of your life or his."

She looked down at the tiny kitten with the huge orange-gold eyes. "Hello. Uh, Thamus, does he have a name?"

"His name will be disclosed to you in time. When you are better able to deal with it, you will receive everything you need to know about him. For now, name him as you would a pet."

She watched the tiny pink tongue lapping at her fingers and felt the scrape of needle-sharp teeth. When he drew back a little, she reached out and grabbed him around his ribs.

"He is so tiny." She couldn't stop smiling as she cuddled him against her.

He let out more of those small and indignant sounds, but a rumbling purr started up as she stroked his small body.

Thamus was shocked when she looked at him. "You made him a kitten."

"Yeah. I always wanted one, but I was never in a home that could have one."

"He is a black kitten."

"Yup. I thought that black had the most dignity."

Thamus pinched the bridge of his nose. "Right. Well, I will register him as your familiar and give you the books you will need to study how to make your partnership more effective."

"Oh, good. I am in the Soul Casting class, and I needed a familiar for that." She rubbed her chin against the top of the kitten's head.

"Contact my office when you have a name for the registry. Naming him will help you focus, and focus will increase your power."

"I will think about it. Can I just go now?"

"Certainly. My assistant will have the

books at the front desk. Pick them up on the way out."

She knew a dismissal when she heard one. Imara got to her feet with her new companion in her arms and left the Master to do whatever he was working on next.

She had her kitten, and he was curled against her and purred happily. Now, she needed the instructions that went along with her new companion.

How difficult could it be?

Chapter Five

"Okay, since you won't answer to an-ything I want to call you, you are going to pick your own name." Imara finished attaching the last sticky note to the wall of her room.

The fluffy black kitten weighed less than a pound as she moved him past the letters. "Just paw the one that you want. I will spell it out."

She moved him past the first layer and in the center of the second; he pawed at the M.

"Right. M. Okay. Next letter." She moved him past the letters again and was becoming despondent when he struck out at the R.

"Okay. M.R. Wait, you want me to call you Mister?" Imara turned him to look at her.

"Mew."

Chuckling, she was going to set him down when he flailed his little paws with their needle-sharp claws at the wall. Either he saw a moth or he wanted to go again.

"Right. Mister. Here we go." She held him and cruised him past the letters again. He attacked the E.

"Meowwwww." He was triumphant.

"Mr. E. Mystery?"

"Mew." He lifted his head high with his paws folded against her fingers.

"Well, either one is better than here, kitty-kitty." She winked at him and set him down.

He scampered away to explore the confines of her room with feet that looked too big for his body. There was a dorky charm to him, as there was to all kittens.

Bara had taken one look at him, squealed and ran out to get him supplies.

Imara had been amused, but Bara was one of those women who really enjoyed cats. Magus Reegar hadn't shown up yet, so it was a question as to how he was going to react to the new arrival.

Imara looked over at the mountain of paperwork, the textbooks she had picked up and the notebooks willing her to fill them. "So, should I study or learn about my people? Decisions, decisions."

Mr. E leaped into the air and landed neatly on the pile of documents. "Mew."

"Well, I am supposed to be following your advice, so sure. Tell me what I should read first."

She eased him from the top of the pile and spread out the folders. The kitten stalked back and forth on them before pawing at one.

Imara opened the file and read the documents inside. The heir contract that needed to produce no more or less than seven sons was detailed as to requirements, and the ability of one or both parties to dissolve it the moment that the seventh living child was born. It included the disposition of any female children to Sakenta. Girls weren't part of the contract. The Demiel family was after a seventh son of a seventh son. They needed an infusion of luck to go with their cash.

The next document was the settlement that Mirrin Deepford-Smythe Demiel had received when she left her husband and children.

The condition of the contract that concerned daughters was rather cold. It was a short addendum that indicated any daughters born to the mother were to be given into care and raised away from the families. No contact between parent and child was to be allowed or encouraged until the daughter in question was an adult.

If more than three daughters were born, the contract was void and both parties would dissolve their union.

Imara sat back and wondered about what would happen if the father engaged in any activity out of the marital union.

A thud got her attention. "What are you up to now, Mr. E?"

Her backpack jerked and twitched. She sighed and finished opening the zipper. A set of rich gold eyes looked up at her from the shadows. "Mew."

She reached in for him, and his little claws hung onto something. The box clattered to the ground a moment later.

Imara blinked. "You wanted me to get that out?"

He waved his paws toward the box.

"Right. This would be easier if you could talk, but I guess I am going to have to work on that."

He gave her a short nod. Nice to know that there was something she was missing. She already felt completely overwhelmed.

Imara picked up the box, and it flared blue in her hands. She nearly dropped it. A small crack appeared along one side of the box, and she used that opening to pry the lid up.

A letter was lying in the box. She slipped it free and examined the heavy parchment and thick seal.

It was addressed to *My Dearest Imara.*

The handwriting was feminine and the seal was that of the Deepford-Smythe family. If she wasn't mistaken, this was a letter from her mother.

She cracked the seal in half and read the letter.

Mr. E crawled into her lap and purred as she sniffled and smiled through the document.

It was simple. If she was reading it, she was an adult and at college. Her mother wanted to start a correspondence with her via the letterbox, but she understood that a student had a lot of pressures in the first few weeks. She could wait until Imara had her feet under her before they met face to face.

Imara carefully folded the letter, and she tucked it into her bag. She wanted it where she could find it if she wanted to read it again.

With a sigh, she picked up Mr. E and rubbed her face into his kitten fur. He started to purr, and she laughed and exhaled hot air onto his skin. He jolted in surprise, and then, his body rumbled violently with the increase of his purr.

She exhaled again, and he went limp in her hands, his eyes blissfully closed.

"What is that?" Reegar floated through the wall and glared at the kitten.

"This is my familiar. His name is Mr. E."

Magus Reegar moved close, glaring at the small bundle of black fluff in her arms.

"He is powerful."

"Apparently. Did you have a familiar?"

"No. I never saw the need. My interest was in potions and spell work, not animal husbandry."

"And bending humans to your will."

He muttered, "That was more of a hobby."

A knock at the door announced Bara with all the cat supplies her vehicle could handle.

"I haven't had so much fun in years." Bara grinned. "I love shopping and finding things. Do you think this is enough?"

"I think it is fine. So, I can use the fridge in the lounge?"

"Of course. Registration is fizzling out. We are on our own for the term. Oh, and I bought him some beef. I hope that's okay. You did say that he could eat people food."

The kitten in her palms came alert at the word beef. He made murping noises and ran to Bara, searching through the bags at her feet.

"And I have lost him. Mr. E, rein in your enthusiasm."

"His name is Mystery? That is so cute."

The look the kitten gave Bara could have curdled milk. It appeared that being cute was an affront to him.

Bara grinned and unpacked several of the bags, setting the food aside so that she could refrigerate it. Toys, a soft bed, a grooming kit and a litter box and litter.

"Wow, you got everything but a toothbrush."

Bara snickered and plunged her hand

into a bag. A toothbrush with a tiny and narrow head emerged. "The toothpaste is flavoured like salmon."

Mr. E popped up on his hind legs and pawed toward the tube.

"Well, I guess I should go to find something to eat and feed him before I organize my books for tomorrow."

He waved his front paws in the air, and Imara snatched him up with one hand while grabbing the bag of food in the other.

Bara remained in her room and started arranging things, humming to herself.

Reegar shook his head and came with them. "She was excited by the idea of an animal in the hall. Apparently, she always wanted a pet."

"You are looking rather fit."

He snorted. "I haven't had this kind of influx of energy in decades. You are very powerful."

"Yup, with no control. It is a lot of fun."

"I can only imagine what it would be like when you were around the dead."

"Well, I was able to make a good living at it just working part time as a death keeper's apprentice." She smiled. "You would be amazed at how much two days a week with the dead can bring."

"Are funds a concern for you?"

"They were. I have enough for now. It will get me though the next few years. After that, I had better find a source of income in short order."

He blinked. "Can you not simply return to your family home and seek a position at your leisure?"

"No. I am an unknown. A discard after a contract. My family and I have no connection. I am truly on my own. I will succeed or fail on my own merits."

"So, it is in your interest to study hard and not engage in the normal frivolity that the college seems to bring out in the young?"

"That is correct. It is the same reason that I got Mr. E. I need him for my courses. A familiar is a prerequisite."

She set the kitten on the floor and unpacked the groceries into the fridge in the lounge. She kept out the enormous steak and set it on the counter.

A little bit of rummaging yielded a cutting board and knife. With practiced motions, she minced up less than a tenth of the meat, segmenting the rest and stowing it in the freezer.

"Here you go. Now, table or floor?"

He made a mewling noise and reached for the small plate.

She scooped him up and put him and the plate on the tabletop. The small smacking noises made her smile as she set about throwing together a quick stir fry for her own purposes.

When Bara appeared, Imara asked,

"Care for some?"

"I could smell it down the hall. I thought you would never ask." Bara got two plates down, and the meat and veg with spices and sauces was split down the middle.

They sat near the fuzzy blob of black that was still making inroads on the beef and shared a meal.

It was her first dinner in her new home, and for the first time in a long time, it felt like she was right where she was supposed to be.

Chapter Six

Sleeping in was not an option. Small, fuzzy paws smacked at her face in a playful staccato.

"Mr. E. Get off."

"Mew."

She sat up and looked out her window. There was no light. "You have to be kidding."

He bounced away, standing next to the door. "Mew."

She grumbled and got out of bed, stumbling to the door. The moment she opened the door, he darted through it, stopped and meowed back at her.

Wearing nothing but a long t-shirt and her panties, she stumbled down the dark hall until she heard the distinct but subtle chime of her alarm. She had left it in the lounge.

"Dammit!" She ran forward and grabbed her phone.

Mr. E jumped up and stood on the table, making little squeaky sounds. She checked the phone and winced at the time. She grabbed him and cuddled him. "Thanks for that. I only lost a few minutes."

He lifted his head proudly. She tickled his head with her fingers and the purr commenced. Time to get ready for class.

Mr. E had an uncanny knack for sitting quietly on her shoulder. The women who saw him cooed and even the men gave him fond looks.

The History of Magic class was full. It was a basic course that could be passed by anyone with a working attention span from elementary school.

Imara announced her name for attendance and didn't have to do anything else but listen to the lectures on the suspected waves of magic and the effect they had had on early man.

Elves were an alteration of human physiology, as were shifters, but it was suspected that mages were exposed over and over before finally absorbing the magic that was being dumped into their geographic location.

Imara took notes, made note of the assignment and got up with the rest of the class. She must have startled Mr. E because he dug his claws in.

She trooped to the dining hall with her compatriots, and she began chatting with a few women who wanted to know about Mr. E. He loved the attention and loved having his own burger and fries for lunch.

Imara opted for a salad and a set of

chicken fingers before she settled in to eat before her familiar could finish his burger.

One of her new companions asked, "So, what can he do?"

She looked at the kitten, who was happily munching away at his meal. "Well, he can put away food at an alarming rate, and he has excellent senses."

He looked at her with a piece of cheese on his little, black nose. "Mew."

The entire table laughed.

She removed the cheese and scratched his head. "Sorry that you got stuck like this."

He gave her a sober look from his bright eyes and slowly nodded.

The frustrations of having the instincts of an infant cat were becoming a secondary memory.

His mage's sincerity was not in doubt. She hadn't betrayed what she knew about him. As far as her companions knew, he was simply a small feline.

He finished the meal she had presented him with and returned to her, cuddling against her chest while she ate. His full belly made him awkward, but he knew she would take care of him if he rested.

One day with his new mage and he still didn't know what she wanted out of life. The others had presented him with a list of demands, but she simply seemed to crave companionship. He could do that merely by remaining the small creature she had chosen him to be.

In all his centuries as a familiar, he had never before had a mage who didn't want to tap into his power immediately. The previous incarnation of servitude had demanded that he start helping with the increase of power immediately and that mage power continued until he died. Eight decades of propelling Magus Yuman Smythe to success in his field of potion design while wearing the body of a raptor had been exhausting. This time, he was actually going to enjoy his punishment. Mage Imara Mirrin had power and no idea what to do with it. If he was careful, he could make her into the strongest mage of her age.

He let out a deep sigh and slumped bonelessly to the table. Life as a kitten might make him small and helpless, but it came with protection offered up by his own mage. It was a strange turn of affairs.

He flicked the tip of his tail lazily as he wondered if there was going to be dessert.

Imara tucked Mr. E into her sweatshirt and zipped it up so she could carry her books. It was time for her Soul Casting class.

When she crossed the college and entered the Wayforth building, she was surprised to find only five other people in the lecture hall.

She was comforted by the fact that all of the other students had an animal with them. It appeared that she was in the right place.

Imara took a seat and settled the unconscious Mr. E into a more comfortable position.

The instructor came out, and the power that surrounded her was stunning. "Hello, I am Magus Deepford, and I am here to teach you how to cast your soul into the universe and bring it home safely again."

The magus's familiar was an elegant

black panther that paced next to her with haughty grace.

"Does everyone have their familiar?" The magus looked around, and her gaze focused on Imara. "Do you have yours?"

Imara unzipped her sweatshirt and pulled out Mr. E. "Got him."

The magus smiled. "Good. He's adorable. Have all of you bonded to your familiars?"

Only one of the students raised their hand.

"Right. Well, we will cover that next week. This week is about the history of familiars. We will cover the reason that we use them and what they can do for us. Once you are aware of the capabilities, you will be tempted to use them. I can assure you that the restrictions of how you can use your familiar are strictly enforced. The Mage Guild hands out punishments to students on a regular basis. They do not make exceptions for youth or inexperience. You will have to take responsibility for everything done using your familiar, no matter its origin."

She looked at the students, one by one, making eye contact and waiting for acknowledgement.

"Now, pull out the textbooks, and we will begin with the first recorded history of a mage using a familiar to extend their own power."

Imara flipped to the first page in the textbook and got her notebook ready. During the lecture, she made notes on things to check up on, including the first familiar and the first hellhound.

The origins of the hellhounds were fascinating. Low-powered mages tapped into the demon zone to increase their energies and ended up bonded to the energies. The bond became genetic after two generations, and after that, there was no going back. Those born to hellhound families were bought, fought and traded amongst the mages until they formed an uprising.

That was the end of the first lecture.

"So, I want you all to identify the players in the uprising and have a list of five ready when we convene again on Thursday. Have a nice two days. Dismissed."

Mr. E had made his way to her shoulder, and he was purring in her ear as she cleared up.

She bagged up her books and slipped her pack over one shoulder. Mr. E adjusted his position, and they left the class in silence.

She wanted to stop and chat, but she had studying to do. There would be time to meet the other would-be mages later.

Bara was at a table in the lounge with her own stack of books. She grinned when Imara staggered in.

"Rough day?"

"I think Mr. E ate his body weight in a cheeseburger and fries."

"You shouldn't let him eat that. He will get sick." Bara was concerned.

Mr. E hopped to the table and flattened himself on the table with a deep purr.

Imara shrugged. "He picked it."

She set her bag down and started pulling out her books and her laptop.

Bara smirked. "Use your student id and the password is ReegarHallRocks."

Imara grinned. "I am guessing we have a fast network?"

"You can stream anything you like. It is wide open, and there is a printer on the network. It is in the kitchenette, next to the fridge."

"I didn't notice it."

"Magus Reegar had it installed. He wants you comfortable." Bara chuckled. "I am enjoying his sudden attention to the modern era."

"I think he just wants to learn to use the internet himself. There is a lot of fey porn out there." Imara grinned as she signed in to the network.

Reegar appeared and took the third seat at the table. "I don't know what that is, but it sounds fascinating."

Bara snorted. "Well, Magus Reegar, I am sure you have seen worse in your time. But, if you want to order a computer, I will help you choose one."

Reegar inclined his head. "Thank you. I will check with the college administration first to see if they can help, but if it doesn't work, I will come to you."

Imara watched as he reached out to pet Mr. E. "You are definitely more solid today."

"Thank you. I feel more alive than I did when I was up and in my own body."

"My pleasure. This used to be my part-time job."

Bara blinked. "How did that work?"

Imara set up her homework station and looked at the RA of Reegar Hall. "Ah, well, I took an aptitude test in high school. I needed an evening job, and Sakenta believes in aptitude application of talent. So, I was assigned to shadow the Death Keepers at the main repository, and a week later, they offered me an apprenticeship at an excellent rate for a teenager. Three years of evenings helping folks speak with their dead managed to pay for college."

"So, you made them stronger?"

Imara sat back and rubbed the back of her neck. "A ghost, or disembodied spirit, loses cohesion over time. If their tether isn't perfect, they will degrade much more quickly. When you have degradation and a strong ghost, you can have all kinds of spectral phenomenon."

She reached down and grabbed a bottle of water from her bag, cracking it open and taking a sip. "My job was to maintain the anchor points that held the tether and warn anyone if they were cracking, clouding or degrading. Speaking to the dead to check their status was part of the job. I thought everyone could make the ghosts stronger when they needed to. Apparently, it is a weird connection that I have to those who are no longer flesh."

"Wow. All I did was mow lawns all summer. Do you have an open mind?"

"Yup, and an open power-generating body. So, I need to find some warding spells or, at least, control."

"I can help you with that. So, did you want to order in or are you willing to try whatever I make in the kitchen?"

Imara smiled. "I am willing to try whatever you come up with. I haven't had much experience with delivery. The boarding house owners didn't want any strangers on their property."

"You are kidding." The woman's astonishment was nearly palpable.

"No. Whatever you choose is fine. I will chip in if you choose delivery." She nodded and got into her books, checking on the assignments and working on her histories.

When Mr. E crept onto her laptop and looked at her with a murp in his voice, Imara cursed and lifted him up, setting him aside and removing the characters he had just created.

"You are no typist, Mr. E. Wow, did you lose weight?"

He murped again and looked smug.

Reegar snorted. "He was fat and then he was thin. He is using his own magic to alter his body."

She picked up her little buddy and cuddled him. "I think he reset himself to summoning specs."

"You know he is powerful."

"I do. It was non-negotiable." She

scratched lightly under the kitten's chin and watched as he closed his eyes, and the purr got louder.

Imara glanced around. "Where is Bara?"

"She went to answer the door. There was a parade of delivery vehicles dropping off parcels."

Imara could feel the prickle of magic as Bara returned with a barrage of bags floating in the air behind her.

"My treat. Pick what you like and we will keep the menus on speed dial." Bara worked her fingers, and a wide blanket covered the floor. Bags opened, plates and cutlery flew around, and in moments, a picnic was ready for a small army.

Bara settled on the floor and waved at the expansive selection. "Take a seat and enjoy. We are the closest thing to sorority sisters that we will have. Consider this a rush party."

Imara had no idea what that was, but she set Mr. E on the ground and settled into the picnic space. "Well, then, sister, shall we dine?"

Chapter Seven

The droning sound woke her for the sixth night in a row. She nudged at the kitten snoring on her abdomen and tried to wake him.

"I told you, you are too small for a pizza." She rubbed his swollen belly.

He squirmed on his back, all four paws in the air. She chuckled and checked the time. It was just after two in the morning.

She sat back and stroked his belly as she pondered her first week of school. The history class was interesting, and she had already prepared all the reports listed on the course outline.

Her financial-planning course was

fun. She enjoyed the numbers and the absolutes of where they went.

Herbology was a tricky course. She had never taken much interest in the properties of plants, but now, it was a lot more than picking the right spices for dinner. She had found that it was taking a lot of her concentration to keep track of what each plant did at what point of the lunar cycle. The possibilities were staggering.

Reegar was surprisingly helpful. He not only had a grasp of herbology, but he also had found the ritual that would ease communication between Imara and her familiar.

The next day in class, in front of everyone and their familiars, she would bind her mind to Mr. E's and finally confirm his identity once and for all.

He could be either Edan Stormborn or Eadric Hellborn. Both led rebellions against the mages regarding the use of demon energy. Both had been brought up on charges when they were captured and disappeared from history.

She had asked the fuzzy monster, but he wasn't telling. He looked smug and then chased his tail the moment she asked. She smiled and laughed instantly, forgetting the question.

Cute and cuddly was the most devastating thing she had come across so far. As she played with him quietly, his eyes opened and he burped. Instantly, he went from roly-poly to his normal slim and dorky.

She chuckled and he got up, curled himself in a ball on her stomach and started sleeping again. He might have been a great and deadly mage, but right now, he was freaking adorable.

Imara settled, made sure her alarm was on and braced for what the next day was going to bring. She was going to do her first, actual, deliberate magic. Was there a word for excitement and eagerness mixed with terror?

"Ms. Mirrin. Are you clear on the protocol?" Magus Deepford checked on their placement in the warded circle.

"Yes. I reach for him and he should reach for me and we meet in the middle."

"Without moving."

Imara sighed. "Right. Ready for this, Mr. E?"

"Mew."

Magus Deepford chuckled. "That is still the cutest damned thing. I have never seen anyone with a kitten for a familiar."

"You haven't?" Imara was suddenly a little nervous.

"No. Most mages pick a more impressive creature as their familiar. Go ahead."

With that resounding endorsement,

Imara looked at Mr. E and reached out with her thoughts. His orangy-gold eyes locked with hers, and she felt a prickle in her mind. The prickle became a tunnel, and soon, she heard thoughts around her that weren't hers.

Welcome to my mind, mage.

Not a mage yet. I am still a Death Keeper's apprentice.

You are much more than that.

So, who do I have the honour of communicating with?

You have narrowed it down to two choices. You are correct. I am indeed one of them.

Which one?

I will let you know at a later date. For now, know that we are indeed bonded until the end of your natural life.

Oh. Goody. Imara sat up straight and nodded to her instructor. "All done."

"Let me just check." Magus Deepford

probed at Imara's mind, and after a surprised jerk, she nodded. "Right. Excellent. Ms. Harkness, you are up."

Ninya Harkness, whose dreams included becoming a captain in a Mage Guild outpost, stepped forward with her hawk, Hector.

Hector eyed Mr. E, but as she gathered her kitten, Imara heard a low growl coming from the tiny body. He wasn't going to back down, and Hector finally looked away.

Impressive.

He always was a lesser mage. Every time I have run into him during my incarceration, he has retreated.

That bore thinking about, but Imara sat back in her seat as Ninya mumbled and chanted, trying to weave the connection.

Imara didn't have to do all the chanting; her skills with the dead were honed enough that she could reach out to another soul who was reaching back.

She cuddled with her buddy as the rest of the class bonded with their creatures.

When the bonding was done, the mage and the beast looked at each other with new eyes.

It was quite jarring when the door to the hall was banged open and a woman strode in toward the front of the class. "Where is Imara..." She checked something written on her wrist, "Mirrin?"

The entire class was staring at the interloper.

Imara got to her feet, and Mr. E hopped to her shoulder. "That would be me."

"You have stolen my familiar."

Imara could feel Mr. E stand up and bristle. "He disagrees."

"I am the Deepford-Smythe heir, and he is mine."

Imara stepped toward her, aware of

their audience. "Could we discuss this in private?"

"No. Claims must be acknowledged by witnesses. He is mine, and I will have him."

Magus Deepford stepped forward. "Laia, this is unseemly. What are you talking about?"

"I went to the familiar center to get my familiar, but the one that was to be delivered to the seventh of seven was already taken. It took a week of bribing and asking the right questions, but I finally found out who got it. She did."

Imara held up her hand before the instructor could speak. "Your birthdate?"

Laia frowned. "What does that have to do with it?"

"Whisper it in my ear. I will tell you mine. I have a right to him if what I suspect is true."

The woman leaned forward and whispered her birthdate. Imara returned the favour with, "Imara Deepford-Smythe out of Mirrin Deepford-Smythe by Desmond Demiel, Seventh of seven by both parties."

Laia blinked and leaned back. "They didn't tell me that."

"I am fairly sure that no one thought of it. Now, do you still have a legitimate claim?"

Laia blushed hot and looked down. "Um, no. I will go and get the next familiar on my family's roster. I apologize for the interruption, cousin."

Imara stared at the pretty blonde with the red face. "It is fine. I can authorize the dean of students to show you the family documentation. If you would leave now, the rest of the students would like to bond with their familiars."

Magus Deepford smiled. "If no one objects, she will need to know how to do this herself. Laia needs to witness the bonding."

Renee and Able nodded that they didn't object, and soon, the class was back in order as the ritual was repeated over and over.

When Magus Deepford addressed them again, she was grinning. "Excellent. Now, next class we will start the beginning focus and rituals of being able to give custody of your soul to your familiar. Dismissed."

Imara exhaled and got to her feet, grabbing her bag. Laia gripped her by the arm. "I am sorry. They just told me that someone else had claimed him. I didn't know about you."

"You still don't. Like I said, I will contact the dean of students and you can look me up."

"Couldn't I just ask you? I mean, we share family."

Imara chuckled. "No, we aren't. I am unknown. I am on record but have never met a relative, until now."

Mr. E let out a small, "Mew." It was a burst of sound that hung in the air between them.

"Mr. E says that it is time for dinner. Would you like to come with us?"

Laia blinked. "Really? I mean, that would be great, but I am meeting some cousins for dinner."

Imara sighed. "Ah. Of course. Another time."

Laia nodded. "Another time. It was weirdly nice meeting you, Imara."

"You too. Good evening." She slung her bag over her shoulder and left the lecture hall. Huh. She had just met her first blood relative face to face. Laia had not spit in her face, so that was something.

The paths between the hall and her classes were burned into her memory. She walked home with a long stride and an urge to talk over what had just happened with Reegar and Bara.

Her mental exercises were stopping the leak of power that she engaged in wherever she walked. The ghosts on the quad stopped rushing at her for power boosts, and she was finally feeling positive about her chances of making it through her first term.

Her Herbology exam was already under way. She had to select six plants that would produce a power and health-enhancing potion when properly enchanted by a master potion maker. That was the exam. She had to pick her herbs that would create the proper potion and drink it herself to test its veracity. There was nothing like putting the pressure on to make sure that the students payed attention.

Ten more weeks and she would know if she had chosen the right herbs and plants or if she was going to turn green and puke.

Reegar was waiting when she came

in. "Congratulations on your bonding! Bara will be late. She left a cake in the cold box."

"She didn't have to do anything. It is my day to cook."

"She wanted to. It was your first spell work. It deserves to be celebrated." Reegar offered her his arm and escorted her into the lounge.

"We didn't do anything. I touched his mind, he touched mine. There is now a tether between us. That's it."

"That tether is going to power everything you do in the next few years. It is an important moment."

"I will trust your judgement on that. You seem perky today."

He chuckled. "I contacted a friend via email. He responded. It has been nearly a century since we last spoke, but he is there and I can talk to him."

"What does he think of your contact?"

"He responded and is on his way here

to meet me." Reegar laughed. "For the first time in a century, I will have a guest that I have actually invited."

"I am excited for you. Did you want me to work on a focus stone?"

"I would rather that you went into the library and charged one of my books. Something personal to me that won't sync itself to other specters."

"Sure. I have a few hours tonight. I am caught up on my homework."

"Good, but first... cake."

Imara giggled and patted his nearly solid arm. "I like the way you think."

Bara came in while Imara was bleeding off her extra energy into a book of masculine erotic etchings from the Victorian era.

"Imara, what are you doing?"

"Giving Magus Reegar a touchstone—of sorts. I mean, I am not going to touch it, but he wanted something to use for emergency power if I wasn't around. He has been so helpful, I said sure."

Bara grinned. "I see you enjoyed the cake."

Imara snorted. "Mr. E decided it had been a while since he had seen cake. He attacked it and is now sulking, after his bath."

Imara looked to her familiar seated on the table and swathed in a wide wrap of towels. He looked like an angry rat, and bathtime had shown her what the communication between mage and familiar could be. There was a lot more cursing on his part than she had imagined. Her mind had been painted scarlet with irritation. He hadn't even let her brush out his fur afterward.

Bara covered her mouth as she giggled. "He looks unimpressed."

"I am unimpressed. That looked like a great cake."

"Aww... you didn't get to have any?"

"Nope. He dropped right onto it without any hesitation."

"Too bad. It was from your family."

Imara paused. "What?"

"Yes. It arrived this afternoon. I didn't have a chance to tell Reegar anything other than that there was a cake in the fridge. He must have assumed I bought it. Congratulations by the way."

"Thanks." The book she was working on glowed softly, and she closed her hand. "I think I am going to do some more studying in my room."

"Don't you want dinner?"

"No. I am fine." She looked at Mr. E and beckoned. "Coming?"

He narrowed his eyes and stalked out of his towel cocoon. She didn't laugh but cuddled him against her chest, picked up his brush and headed for their room.

Family had sent the cake. It reminded her of the box and the letter she had yet to write.

I am sorry I ruined your cake. I just had the urge to jump so I did.

It is fine. Cake can be distracting. You did remind me of something, though.

What was that?

I need to write to my mother. Sulking about my situation won't make it better. Only by taking action can I change my circumstance.

You got all that from my leap into icing?

It was a very profound leap.

He pressed his head against her shoulder, and she brushed him out until his black fur was silky and smooth once again. When he was asleep in her lap and she was seated at her desk, she pulled out sheets of paper and began to compose a letter to her mother.

She scrapped several drafts before beginning the letter with, *Dear Mother. I performed my first conscious magic today.*

Imara took a deep breath and kept writing.

Chapter Eight

Two days after the bonding, Imara got another parcel. She got back from her herbology class and found a box on the step outside Reegar Hall.

"Weird. Huh, it's for me." She flipped the box in her hands and noted the popular website logo on the packing tape.

Mr. E thudded on top of it a moment after she turned it around. *Notgood, notgoodnotgood. Don't touch.*

"What?"

Get Reegar. Mr. E was perched on the box, fully fluffed with his back arched.

Imara frowned, but she entered the hall and called out, "Magus Reegar, I need some assistance here."

Reegar walked toward her, smiling brightly. "Imara. How lovely. My guest was wanting to speak with you."

"That sounds delightful, but first, I need your help. There is a parcel on the doorstep, and Mr. E won't let me near it."

Reegar scowled and walked to the door. He opened it and looked down at the angry, miniscule cat and the box he was standing on.

"Well, I can't do anything myself, but the timing is very lucky. Let me get my guest."

Imara stood with her pack on her shoulder, looking at the box with the new accessory made of fur. "Right. Thank you."

A moment later, Reegar walked down the hall with a creature made of shades of grey and silver.

The elf was dressed in rich charcoal tunic and trousers with a wide sash at the waist. The boots were matte, and if he stood in the shadows, he would nearly disappear. Well, most of him. The silver of his hair blazed like a beacon.

"It is an honour to meet you, Imara Mirrin."

She inclined her head. "I will return the greeting as soon as we get the parcel sorted so my familiar can engage in his normal evening food orgy."

Reegar pushed her back against the wall with a gentle hand on her shoulder. "Don't touch it. Liirick will take care of it. Won't you, Lee?"

"This is a nasty piece of spell work. Did you handle it?"

She looked at her hands. It had been a cold day, so she was wearing gloves. "By the corners."

The elf knelt and used the edges of his sleeves to lift the box and the familiar up, bring it within the building. "Ree, where is your lab?"

"Follow me."

Magus Reegar led the way down a hall that he had pronounced strictly off limits to her until she was a second year.

"So, you are Liirick of the Dark Shadows?" Imara trailed behind them.

"I am. You may call me Lee."

"I just finished a report on you for my history class. I had no idea you knew Reegar."

"He and I were friends for all of his years. I was a guest lecturer here, and he and I met socially after. The Guild was not pleased, but he remained my steadfast companion whenever I was in town."

The relationship and Reegar's delight in being physical gave her sudden understanding. "I am glad you were able to reconnect."

Lee glanced at her, and she noted that his eyes were a dark pewter and they twinkled with amusement that belied his age. He was over six hundred and had come in to help many human settlements when the waves of magic broke and spread across the world like ripples in a pond. He had helped them adjust and trained the mages that had gone from simple lives to being able to manipulate the world around them. Fey and mages like him had saved lives and helped get the one-percent mages to safety.

"So, you wrote a report on me?"

"Yes, well, you were one of the mages I focused on. Having folk like you finding the single mages in larger communities and getting them to safety is what made the Guild possible." She held her breath.

"Yes?"

"What is a wave like? There hasn't been one in decades."

Lee grinned. "I think that can wait until after I disable this curse."

"Oh. Right. Is that what that is?"

"Yes. It is keyed to your blood, so as long as you don't make contact with it, it is fine for me to handle. You were lucky I was here."

She wrinkled her nose as they entered the lab. "Yeah, I have that kind of luck."

Lee set the parcel down on a worktable, and he got forceps and blades.

Mr. E scampered over to the edge of the table, so Imara let him resume his post on her shoulder.

Reegar went to a cabinet on the wall, and he opened it, removing a few bottles of coloured liquids before walking over to the table and setting them down.

"Thank you, Reegar." Lee smiled briefly and began the careful work of slicing into the box.

Imara pulled up a chair and watched the procedure from several feet away.

The box was opened; the folded paper that had kept it in place was carefully removed and set into a large copper bowl.

"Hmm, I would guess that this is a fourth-level charm and not the first curse that this person has sent. The blood that has marked it is strange."

Imara perked up as Lee gave a running description. "Strange?"

"It is your blood, but it is male. It has to have come from a close relative, but the strange thing is that the blood itself is the curse. I have nev—wait, I have seen this once before. Do you have siblings?"

She wrinkled her nose. "Several. At least seven."

"How many cousins?"

"I have no idea. I met one a few days ago. She seemed nice."

"This is definitely male blood. An unlucky child."

Imara went cold and then hot. "You don't say."

"Yes. This kind of charm only works with the blood of an unlucky one. So, your brother's blood mixed with that of the cursed blood from the same family and you have an excellent curse."

He used the forceps to lift out a small bundle of fabric marked with glyphs. He set it into the bowl, on top of the paper. With the contents of the box disposed of, he shredded the box and set it in the bowl around the edges.

"You must be hell on Christmas presents." Imara observed.

Lee grinned and Reegar chuckled. "He brings the surgical kit to the tree."

Lee sighed. "I have not celebrated the holidays since you passed, Reegar."

Reegar's form fluctuated as he was overtaken with emotion.

Lee carefully unstoppered the bottle with blue solution, and he drizzled it over the contents of the bowl. "This is a negating solution. It takes apart the blood on a cellular level and is not something you want to touch to your skin."

A dark bottle with an arcane label was opened next. "This will attract the curse and hold it so we can destroy it."

"Right. Makes sense."

A single drop fell from the bottle, and Lee stepped back as a stream of flame shot upward.

"Got it. Imara, can you light a match?"

He was standing with his hands to either side of the bowl, so she struck the match.

"Now, insert the match so the flame is above the blue stream of fire."

She followed his direction and eased the eighteen-inch wooden match past his hands and into the small flame in the center of the bowl. The explosion was sudden, and Lee grabbed her and put his body between her and the violent explosion.

Imara hadn't seen a magical shield before, but she was wrapped in one as the echoes faded. She looked down to the generator of the shield, and her kitten looked at her soberly.

I told you it was dangerous.

Thank you.

I do not wish to see your promising career end quickly. I have faith in your ability to be a great and troublesome mage.

She grinned and scooped him up, cuddling him.

"Thank you as well, Liirick. You have a lot of skill at unraveling curses."

He chuckled. "I have been taught by the best. The DeMonstres are friends that I spend a lot of time with."

Reegar set about cleaning up after the explosion. "Well, this is not how I anticipated your first visit, Lee."

Lee moved to the specter and wrapped his arms around him. "I came to see you. Whatever comes up, I am just delighted to be visiting."

Imara smiled and returned to the entryway, gathering her backpack and hoisting Mr. E to her shoulder.

She carefully removed her gloves and tossed them in the trash.

The tea party set in the lounge was amazing. Reegar had gone all out.

The specter and the elf returned to the lounge, and Liirick poured her a cup of tea.

The steam was disconcerting. "How can it still be hot?"

"I have educator status at this college. I have free rein to use magic for any purpose. That includes keeping the tea hot and the sandwiches cold. They are from a bakery in town that has been around since the start of the college. It was a trip through nostalgia to come back here."

The elf prepared a plate for her and

extended his arm. "For your valiant defender."

Mr. E murped proudly and hopped to the table, diving into the sandwiches with his amazing appetite.

"He eats on the table?"

She smiled. "When he can make the jump from the floor to the table without magic, he can eat down there. Until then, he eats where I can keep an eye on his intake."

"You are worried about his diet?"

Imara chuckled. "No, I am fascinated by how much he can eat."

Lee sat back and Reegar joined them. "What are you two discussing?"

"Mr. E's eating habits."

"Ah, a fascinating subject. I have never observed a familiar eating as much as he does or eating human food, for that matter. But, I have not actually met an inherited familiar with a penal aspect."

Mr. E growled at him. Apparently, he

was sensitive about that designation.

"I don't care what they say about him. So far, he has been a great familiar. Doesn't even peek on me in the shower."

He continued to devour a thin ham sandwich.

Lee chuckled and Reegar sat next to him. Their hands were close on the table. It was sweet.

Reegar sighed. "This was my favourite bakery. I will miss the flavours."

Imara blushed a little, but she felt it necessary to say, "Have you tried skelping?"

Reegar blinked. "What?"

Liirick cocked his head. "What is that?"

"It is a slang term for possession for pleasure. Reegar would place his specter within your body, and what you can experience, he can experience. It isn't just electrical impulses that give a simulation of life but uses a living body to feel. You have to agree, of course. You could propel him outward in a moment if you didn't. Life always wins.

Reegar looked to his ex-lover and raised his brows. "If you were willing, I would love to try, but I am a little too solid for that."

She coughed delicately. "Bleed off your extra energy into metal or stone. You will be intangible once again."

Lee was grinning. "You want to be inside me?"

Reegar chuckled. "In the worst way."

Imara reached for a plate and picked out a few sandwiches. "If you two are going to get reacquainted in public, I am going to grab some snacks and head to my room. I will be back for Mr. E in a moment. Don't do anything of the naked variety until then, please."

Reegar held up his hand. "Do not leave. Aside from our flirting, Lee has too many manners to make a lady feel uncomfortable."

Lee shrugged. "He is not wrong. You are here for the next three years. That is plenty of time to play at our leisure. I can probably arrange three or four lectures per term and come in on weekends around that schedule."

Imara blinked. "I think I would like to attend some of those lectures."

"You might not be able to attend until you complete your first term, but I can always let you know what you missed in a private tutorial."

"That sounds pleasant. I would like to know how to recognize a cursed object. I had no idea what you saw when you looked at the box."

Lee looked at her and cocked his head. "You are warded."

"Yeah, I had to do it to stop the leak."

"It is the wrong type of ward for you. Instead of helping you, it has blinded you. If Reegar will assist, I can make you a charm that will appear the same from the outside but leave your senses free.”

Mr. E got up and walked over to sit in front of Reegar.

“Lee, what is he doing?”

The rumbling purr and sudden rise to his hind legs made Imara cover her laugh with her hand.

Reegar's voice was strangled. “What is he doing?”

Lee smirked. “He is giving you big kitten eyes.”

“Spells and stars, that is adorable. Yes, yes, of course I will help.”

With a cheerful murp, he turned and trotted back to his plate. Imara covered her face and howled with laughter. It was nice to know that it wasn't just her that he could wrap around his fluffy paw.

Chapter Nine

The letter exchange with her mother became a regular feature of her life, but she had to cut back after midterms. She hadn't done as well as she had hoped, and there had been two more cursed boxes on the doorstep. Reegar had called an instructor to take care of the parcels, and the person leaving them had yet to be identified.

The small amulet she wore tucked into her bra was preforming exactly as Lee had described. She could see out, but they couldn't see in. Her stray energies were also contained but that was more meditation and practice than anything else.

"Enough, Imara. You have been studying for weeks; you are ahead of everything except Herbology, and you need to get out and have some fun."

She looked at Bara briefly and turned back to the textbooks and research books on the history of magic. Reegar had brought in more books from somewhere, and she hadn't had to spend any time in the college library.

"I don't need fun. I didn't budget for fun."

"I will pay. There is a fey orchestra playing in the quad tonight."

Imara smirked. "That is a lie. It is a goblin rave. I might have my head in my books, but I did look up and see the posters."

"Half-goblins. Their voices are supposed to be incredible."

"Why does it have to be tonight? I was just getting in-depth on the third century when that wave hit. It is the first recorded instance of trolls and giants."

"Fascinating. Come out and have fun. Just for a few hours, you can pretend to be a normal student. Come on..." Her whine was what did it.

"Fine. Fine. I will come with you, but I am wearing this. Oh, and Mr. E."

Bara frowned. "I don't know if he will like the sound."

Imara saw the logic in that. "Mr. E, do you want to go to a goblin concert?"

He gave her a slow blink and rested his head on his paws. He was content where he was, sleeping on her backpack and guarding her snacks.

"So, that's a no. Well, I guess I can spare an evening."

She looked at her paperwork and memorized what was where.

Once she had a good idea of where she had left off, she stacked everything together and brought it to her room. She returned to the lounge, and Bara appeared surprised. "Ready?"

"Sure. I am not going for socialization, so makeup is not necessary. This is an open party, so a skirt isn't necessary. I am fine in jeans and a sweatshirt."

"Right. Okay, come on, dinner is on me."

Imara grinned and gave herself a quick pat down to find her wallet. She had her ID, so she was all set.

"Excellent. Lead on."

Bara linked arms with her and hauled her out of their home and into the night.

They made their way to the gathering throng, and Imara grinned. "Food carts."

"Well, I am not taking you to the dining hall. Come on, those little donuts are calling me."

Grinning, Imara went to experience the depths of junk food before she stood and listened to her first concert.

Sharing small portions with Bara was

surprisingly fun.

"So, why did you choose Reegar Hall?" Imara mumbled it around a mouthful of fries, cheese and chili.

"Same reason as you. Finances. Reegar Hall needed a resident advisor to continue to be considered part of the college, and I needed a place to live when my original hall was over capacity."

"That can happen?"

"Sure. I was on a waiting list for housing and told to check in when I arrived. When I arrived, Leethan Hall was full and I was out on my ass. The housing advisor recommended my asking for a placement at Reegar Hall, and Magus Reegar agreed. I had a place to live and a master mage to point me in the right direction when he was feeling sociable. It has been a comfortable few years, though I haven't been able to get any folks to come over for an evening. No one is interested in dealing with him."

"He seems pretty cheerful to me."

"He has been able to interact with the physical world for the first time in nearly a hundred years. Of course he is cheerful." Bara snorted. "Seriously, though. I am happy that you signed up for us. I was spending more time in the library than at home, and I love the library at the Hall."

"It is thorough. I like studying there. It is so quiet and Reegar is very helpful."

Bara moved closer to her, "Is there any progress on your stalker?"

"Is that what it is? I thought I had a personal terrorist or a mail-order assassin." Imara grinned. "The afterlife isn't too bad, and Mr. E would get to get another mage assigned to him."

Bara was shocked. "You hold your life so cheap?"

"No, but I am not afraid of what happens next after we leave the physical world. Specters are just another phase of existence."

Bara tossed the empty container and wiped her hands on a napkin. She flicked her fingers, and flame took the napkin.

"I wish I could do that." Imara sighed.

"It is a third-year spell."

"Excellent. I have passed a few of the equivalency exams, so I am going to start using the fun stuff after this term." Imara looked around and watched the variety of humans mixing and mingling in the quad. The band was setting up and getting ready to start their set. Imara had never seen a goblin in person before, but only two of them were pure.

The four-armed drummer was practicing a few beats; the six-eyed keyboardist was checking his equipment and the two nearly human guitarists were in conversation. The base player was human. Well, he was mostly human.

His skin was greenish and his ears were pointed.

Bara murmured as they joined the crowd. "What equivalencies?"

"I am a third-degree necromancer, second-degree enchanter and first-degree potion master." Imara grinned. "I had some time on my hands before the exams."

"How long are you planning to be in school?"

"Three years or less. I need to get out and make a living." She shrugged.

"Wow. That is quite the career path. What do you want to do?"

"I want to get into necromancy or possibly the spectral arts." She grimaced. "I have to decide soon. The next thing I know I am going to be out of my first term and I will have to make up my mind."

"I thought you had more of a budget for classes than that."

"I have enough for five years, but I don't want to spend that time here."

"Why not?"

"Because that money will get me an apartment and a wardrobe to start a new life. Mr. E eats a lot."

They had to stop their discussion because the band started the concert, and Imara was rapidly going deaf with a grin on her face.

An hour later, her hearing was a thing of the past, but she was still smiling. The music had moved her and had decided her on one of the courses she wanted to tackle. If there was still space, she wanted to take Sound Magic Theory. She wanted to know how someone could move her with just sound, strings and a beat.

They were near Reegar Hall when she was struck.

A shadow separated from a nearby

hedge and charged for her. There was a body behind the shadow as it collided with her. Pain shot into her arm, and the impact dropped her into Bara. They fell to the ground, and everything went scarlet.

Bara was yelling and trying to get her to sit up. Imara helped as much as she could, and Mr. E met them on the way to the Hall.

He climbed her body while Bara was walking her to the building, and he tasted the impact spot on her arm.

She is going to die.

Imara couldn't answer. She was wracked with agony as Reegar took over her maintenance, lifting her into his arms and carrying her to the lab.

It took twenty minutes of Reegar barking orders and Bara applying a series of treatments in turn, for Imara to be able to speak.

She could feel the fury of Mr. E in her

blood. He was on the hunt. "Mr. E is hunting."

"I am glad you are back with us. I have managed to reduce the effect of the poison, but I have had Bara put a call in to the main office. Unfortunately, there are several idiots who are taking up the healers that you need. We can't identify the toxin completely without them."

"Threbesh demon blood. They stabbed me with demon blood." She gritted her teeth and relayed what Mr. E was telling her.

Reegar sighed. "Good. That is an easy fix. Where is he? He should be with you."

She closed her eyes as Reegar started barking out orders to Bara. She sought out Mr. E, but he was busy. His mind was full of rage and ancient hate.

She opened her eyes as Bara applied a poultice that smelled like sulfur and mint. "Uh, Mr. E is busy right now."

Eadric the Hellborn crouched low to the ground as he faced down his opponent.

You think that that feeble body can take me, Eadric? I have waited centuries for you to be given a form that matched your skills.

Eadric circled to get an attack position on the ferret with the bad attitude. *I see your mage chose a form that matched your soul. I have rarely seen a better match to personality, Kemeer.*

So, you recognized me? I thought I had managed to hide rather well. The idiot who inherited me was easy to control.

That is not our place, Kemeer.

It is what I want. I have used her to gain what I needed to destroy your mage, and when her heart beats her last, you will be returned to wait for decades until you can be assigned to the next generation. In the meantime, I will gather power and bring the mages back to the top of the food chain.

That is why you were made a familiar in the first place, Kemeer. He growled and gathered himself.

Eadric felt a surprising burst of power coming from Imara, and he used it to effect.

Kemeer may have thought he was getting a kitten, but in a wave of energy, Eadric took on the body of a black tiger, stepping calmly on the small, squirming body until it cracked.

The woman sitting in the corner, dressed in black and holding a blade, came to her senses. "What? Kimmy, where are you?"

Eadric resumed his kitten form and left the way he had come. Kemeer wasn't dead, but he was crippled. He would need attention, and there was only one place his mage could take him.

Eadric bolted back to Reegar Hall to be with his mage while she recovered. He wasn't sure if she even knew that she had sent her strength to him.

The door to the hall cracked open at his approach, and he streaked toward the lab without hesitation.

Imara was slumped in a chair, face pale, lips blue, while Bara was working on her. The young mage applying medical assistance was crying. "It isn't working."

Eadric hopped up onto Imara's lap, and he pressed his head against her ribs. His purr was deep, and he hoped that it was enough. He put all of his power into his mage and tried to stop the leeching of her soul through her open wound.

Hey fuzzy guy. Did you get it done?
He is incapacitated.
Why?

He sighed against her chest. *He hates me. He is one of those I was fighting against, and his crimes against the unpowered populace landed him in the inherited-familiar system.*

So, he kills me and he sends you back to storage?

And he has a clear run at bringing the mages back to power. That is his end goal. He considers mages to be superior to pretty much everyone else.

He could hear Bara muttering, "It is working."

So, who was he?

The familiar to the receptionist at the familiar facility. He saw me the moment you carried me to the desk to get the materials.

Does his mage know?

No. He had her within his control. She was the one who attacked you. When she takes him in for medical care, we will learn where she got the blood for the curses.

I will let Reegar and Bara know. What was the name of the familiar?

Kemeer. His mage calls him Kimmy. He is a ferret.

Right. I hope I can enunciate. Her chuckled in their link made him relax a little. She was a good mage and had the potential to be a great one.

Imara lifted her head. "Person responsible is a ferret named Kimmy. Kemeer the archmage is the familiar of the receptionist at the familiar center. He hates Mr. E and has been taking control of his mage in order to kill me and destroy Mr. E for this generation."

Bara looked at Imara, "Familiars don't take control of their mages."

"This one does. Read your history.

Kemeer wanted to raise the mages above all others, and he was willing to use whatever he could to accomplish it. Demon-zone energy was one of those things." She spoke in a rush. She could feel darkness pushing in on her again.

"Right. We need to get you to the infirmary, but I can't carry you."

"Get me on my feet. Mr. E will help me walk there. This can't be done in the darkness. If I am not coming out of it, I want to make sure there are witnesses to my death that will record it. If it is Kemeer, he needs to be stopped."

She squirmed out of Bara's hold and sat on the edge of the chair. With a few deep breaths, she levered herself to her feet; Mr. E was draped around her neck, still purring.

Bara was frowning. "You need to sit. I am sure they will be here soon."

"I am not. I will walk toward the infirmary, and if they turn up here, Reegar can tell them where to go." She took a slow step and then another. Reegar watched over her as she moved at a slow pace toward the door.

Reegar finally announced. "I am not going to let you die on the lawn. Hold tight to Bara when you step out the door."

His words were weirdly ominous, but Bara stepped to her side and held her hand as they stepped across the threshold.

A tunnel of light rushed to greet and engulf them. When the light faded, they were standing in the entry hall of the infirmary.

The folk waiting to be seen were drunk, drugged or had minor fight injuries.

Bara tried to get someone's attention, but Imara had used up all her strength. She sagged against Bara, sliding toward the ground.

A deafening roar made all the conversations stop.

Imara smiled as the noise repeated and she hit the floor. In seconds, hands lifted her up and Bara was explaining the situation and the initial treatment that had been administered. She was rushed past the waiting area and into treatment.

"So, you had excellent urgent care, Ms. Mirrin. The idea was right, but the ingredients were no longer effective. They had degraded over time and could only give partial relief."

The healer at her side made notes in her chart. "We don't often see blood poisoning of this variety, but your friend was able to direct me to a familial match on campus. He agreed to donate a few pints for you."

A shadow fell between her and the light. A male voice chuckled, "And they didn't even give me a cookie."

The healer cleared his throat. "I will leave you to get acquainted."

She glanced to her left, and an IV drip was still providing her with blood. "I am guessing that you are one of the Demiel men?"

He extended his right hand to hers. "I am Luken Demiel. I believe we are twins."

"Imara Mirrin, and yes, we are."

"You know, it was the strangest thing. I was in the waiting room with a buddy who had picked a fight with the drummer from the concert and a woman came out and asked if there were any Demiels around. I raised my hand, and the next thing I know, I found out you needed help and I volunteered."

"Just like that?"

He carefully settled on the edge of the bed. "Well, your familiar did put his claws to my throat and growl at me. I got the feeling that he would have taken the blood by force if he had to."

Imara looked around and saw Mr. E, sitting watchfully on her thighs, his tail flicking.

"I have never been threatened by a kitten before. It was an interesting experience." He smiled.

She saw an echo of her own face in Luken's. "He's an interesting individual."

"I can see that. He is an inherited familiar?"

"He is. Our mother's side of the family wasn't fussy about gender when it came to the seventh child."

Luken nodded. "My career path doesn't require a familiar, so you are welcome to him. He is a little runty for my taste anyway."

Mr. E got up on his tippy toes and hissed.

Imara extended her hand to him and

stroked his fur, careful of the IV. "He is exactly what I needed, exactly when I needed him."

His mind touched hers, and she reciprocated. She chuckled. "I wouldn't have it any other way."

Chapter Ten

Exams rushed in around testifying and having Mr. E examined from nose to tail. Imara spent most of her time in the lounge and library.

Reegar had been visited by every necromancer in four counties, but none had been able to figure out how a man dead for nearly a century had created a gateway across the campus. It should not have been possible, but then, they didn't take into account that Imara had charged up every bit of gay erotica in the building with enough power to make him nearly corporeal. That was a lot of erotica, but it had taken the heat off her activating ghosts on the campus.

Weeks of carefully nurturing her plants was now down to the final exam. Imara carried the tray of plants into the exam room along with the other students. The normal jovial atmosphere was tense.

Their instructor examined their trays and confirmed that the herbs they were holding were theirs and theirs alone. Each plant was tagged, each tag was enchanted and each pot was warded. They were as secure as they could be.

"When we started prepping for this exam, I told you that the goal was to create a formula to enhance power and health. Two of you have most of the proper ingredients. The rest of you are going to have an interesting day."

Imara stood by her workstation as the door to the class opened and fifth-level potion masters walked in with their mortars and pestles.

"Al right, students. Pick the ingredients in the correct quantity and hand them to the potion master."

The woman in front of her had quirked lips.

Mr. E started to whisper in her mind, and she followed his direction, plucking only a few leaves off each plant, holding them together before plucking more.

When they were done, she inhaled the fragrance and thought about it. Mr. E was silent.

She needed more mint. Her power ran hot, and she needed cooling.

Her potion master was grinning as Imara put the ingredients in the bowl. "Go to it, madam."

Imara's was the last potion master to get to work, but she muttered and whispered quickly. She was the first finished. "Done."

She took the mortar and tipped it, dripping the liquid into a vial. There was barely a handful of drops in it.

The potion master corked the potion and handed it over. "There you go. Good luck."

Imara set the small bottle in front of her, and she waited for the rest of the class to finish. The instructor came to her, opened the vial and nodded. "Exit the classroom and go to the left. When you are there, you will be taken to a cubicle where you can take your potion."

"Yes, Magus." She nodded and took the vial, holding it in her fist so no one could see how small the sample was. As she passed others, there were huge salads of herbs being crushed into potions.

She had her tiny sample, and she hoped it was enough of the right things.

Out the door to the left, there was a fey with familiar features and more behind him. He winked and gestured for her to be quiet.

"Come with me, student."

She followed him to a cubicle, and he

gestured for her to take a seat on the lounge while he perched on a high stool. "Take your potion whenever you are ready, student."

She dragged in a deep breath and un-corked the vial. She was about to tip it toward her lips when she paused. Not all herbs were designed to be taken inter-nally. Two of them were in her potion. She turned to the scar on her arm from the stabbing, and she poured the drops onto that mark. She rubbed it in and washed her hands with the last of it. A bright tingle ran through her fingers and worked in her arm. Heat and power started to pulse in her veins, and she sighed deeply. "That feels better. I was starting to feel it when it rained."

"Pass. You have passed your Herbol-ogy course with a Excel grade. You are now able to take any mage or potion courses in the future."

"Why?"

"Because you know how to listen to the plants and be wary of what they can do. Ignoring basic chemistry is how most potion mages suffer injuries. So, you are free to go. Enjoy the power and the health."

"It will only last a few weeks."

He grinned. "The power, yes, but the health and any repairs made to your body will remain. Your arm looks much better."

She glanced down at the stab wound, and her eyes watered when she could only see the faintest outline of the blade mark and that was still fading.

"Right. Thank you, observer. Have a good day." She nodded and passed him, walking down the hall that he directed her to.

Behind her, she heard an explosion and shouting, so she was guessing that one of the other students wasn't getting a top grade.

Whew. Thanks for the guidance.

I was only reiterating what you had been practicing. Quantity doesn't mean more power, it just means less control. You knew that. You just needed reminding during the practical application.

Mr. E purred into her ear, and she giggled. *Why do you do that?*

It is why you chose this form for me. You need comfort, and a kitten is the best means to deliver it. I have no problem with that.

Your ego can handle it?

My ego can handle a lot.

Good to know. She left the Herbology building and headed for home. She had one more exam to study for, and it was going to make or break her career options.

Soul manipulation seemed to be what she was designed for, so she wanted to get an Excel in the Soul Casting course. It was simple; she had to park her anchor in Mr. E and send her soul to one part of campus, retrieving information that would only be found at that spot. Once she had it, she needed to return to her body and tell the class what she had seen.

She was going to need to practice a few times more if she wanted to be able to stuff herself back in her body with any kind of speed. Her issue was extra energy and bleeding it off in an appropriate manner.

Bara and Reegar were helping her practice, and Luken even came by now and then to lend a hand. Their relationship was a strange one, but they were both making careful strides to knowing each other.

If Imara didn't know better, she would think that Luken and Bara were developing more than a casual relationship. She grimaced. It was a brain bender for another time. If they did get together, it wasn't her business.

That night, she was going to scatter herself around the campus and try to stuff herself back into her body in under five minutes. This was going to require pizza, lots of pizza.

"Ms. Mirrin, you are up." Magus Deepford tapped a folded document against her open hand.

Mr. E was at full attention on her shoulder. He was ready.

Imara took the stage, and she knelt in the control circle. Magus Deepford handed her the document. "Whenever you are ready."

Mr. E jumped to his spot in the circle, directly in front of her, and he nodded.

She cracked open the seal on the exam, and it said, *Find the person in scarlet on the third floor of the administration building and read their nametag.*

She nodded to the teacher and stated,

"Start the clock."

She locked her gaze to her familiar's, parked her soul with him and took the rest of her mind on a journey through the campus.

She found the offices on the third floor and flashed along until she located the man wearing the scarlet shirt with the nametag. She chanted the name to herself as she turned and headed back to the Wayforth building.

Her excitement had charged her, so she activated a few ghosts that Reegar had enticed for this purpose. They caught the extra energy and had a physical presence for a few hours, but it let her squeeze back into her body, pulling the link back from Mr. E's protection and opening her eyes.

She wrote the answer for the instructor, her hand shaking. When it was done, she handed the paper over and said, "Time."

Magus Deepford stopped the clock. "Forty-five seconds. Well done, Ms. Mirrin. Well, that is well done if you have the right answer."

She looked at the answer and chuckled. "*U R Name* is the correct answer. Most students choose the woman in red, by the way."

"It said scarlet, I went for scarlet."

"I can confirm the well done. You have passed with an Excel grade."

Imara's shoulders slumped in relief. "Thank you."

"Don't thank me. Now, get out of here. It is time for the next student. Mr. Dillwell, please take the stage."

Mr. E jumped to her shoulder, and she resumed her place next to the others who had completed their exams. A few discreet high fives went around before Dillwell finished his exam. He did it in three minutes and forty-five seconds. It was a passing grade, and his relief was evident.

Ninya turned to her and asked, "We are going out to celebrate after this. Will you join us?"

Imara grinned. "I would love to but have some friends that I am getting together with. Thank you for the invitation; I am looking to be more sociable in the second term."

She said her farewells and listened to Mr. E's triumphant whoops and chortles as she left the lecture hall and headed for the open air.

She had passed. Every first course had been passed with high marks. She was ready for the new courses of the second term. She was a giant leap closer to her new life and being giddy with relief didn't cover it.

She could hear the pounding of the music before she even reached Reegar Hall. The drab, grey building was pulsing with energy, and when she entered the familiar space, the laughter and high emotion of the specters she had over-charged was everywhere.

Bara greeted her at the door. "I am guessing that you passed?"

Imara nodded and hugged her friend. "I passed!"

"Good, then we aren't throwing this party for nothing." Bara hauled her into the lounge where Reegar and Lee were hosting a modest buffet with a huge *Congratulations* banner over their heads.

Luken walked toward her with a huge cake in his hands, a tiny sculpture of Mr. E had been depicted in sugar. A pathway had been drawn on the cake and the first five blocks after the start block had been marked with her grades. The end of the path was twenty marks away, and she dragged in a deep breath.

"Wow. Thank you." She kept her senses trained on Mr. E, but he didn't seem inclined to leap on this particular cake.

"Well, blow out your familiar and we can tuck in."

She giggled and leaned forward to blow out the candle protruding from the kitten sculpture.

When the small plume of smoke curled upward, the specters and her friends cheered. Luken set the cake down and the party began in earnest.

Reegar and Lee started the dancing off, engaging in the moves of Swing as if they had danced together a thousand times before.

Imara kept the power flowing to the party as she sat and had cake with Luken and Bara.

"So, Luken, you are a third year?" She smiled at him.

He blushed. "How did you know?"

"Your aura. You have the mark of learning on you, but it is the mark made by picking up knowledge you didn't particularly want. Mandatory classes."

"Aura?"

"Well, soul print is more the thing. I can see power, emotion, energy, but only in a few situations when I concentrate."

"Wow. Nice. I wish I had something like that. I am stuck with standard spell casting."

Bara perked up. "Really? What is your favourite spell?"

Imara eased away from them with her fork busy providing her with all the cake she could want. It was damned good cake.

The ghosts were having a rave, and she was right in the middle of it. A few came to say thanks for the moment of clarity and others questioned her on her family lines. She found polite comments for all of them and eased out of the hall, taking in the evening air.

"It sounds like quite a party in there."

Imara looked at the woman standing in the shadows. "It is. Would you like to come inside?"

"I have not been invited."

Imara grinned. "It is my party; I am inviting you now."

"What is it for?"

"I survived my first term at the college with excellent marks. If I can maintain it, I can fast track myself into a career in a couple of years."

The woman tilted her head. Imara still couldn't see her.

"Is it wise to rush an education?"

Imara chuckled. "I won't stop learning just because I graduate. I will simply have the prerequisites to pay my own way in the world. I need to work, and I want to work, but I have to get credentials to be able to do what I want to do."

"You are a young woman with a path in her mind. Is that your familiar?" The laughter in her tone was unmistakable.

"Mr. E, this is a strange lady in the shadows. Strange lady, my name is Imara and this is Mr. E." She could feel Mr. E stretching from his comfy spot draped around the back of her neck. He made a cute murp sound, and the woman chuckled.

"I am the Chancellor of Depford College. My name is Mirrin Deepford-Smythe. I am your mother and very glad to see you."

Imara stared at the face that looked like she would in thirty years. "I am pleased to meet you."

"Ah, my baby girl. You have no idea how happy I am to finally be able to touch you." She extended her hand and Imara took it.

The delivery room, fighting to hold her daughter and announcing to her husband that their contract was at an end. The rush of emotions was intense and bittersweet. She knew that Imara would be fine. She had the luck of two families behind her. She would grow strong, and when she was an adult, Mirrin would find her again.

Imara staggered when her mother released her hand. "You gave me your memories."

"I did. It was faster than explaining."

"I think I get it. The Deepford-Smythes are broke?"

"Not now, not anymore. You brought luck to the family line the day you became a death keeper."

She thought back. "Is that why the Dean of Students came on my first day?"

"Yes, your great-great aunt sent a letter and entailed her unclaimed estate to you. Didn't they tell you?"

"No. It wasn't mentioned in the documents."

"Ah, well there is a trust that will kick

in when you graduate. It is a nicely sized bit of funds with a chunk of property in downtown Redbird City. Is that really the fearsome familiar?"

Mr. E lifted his head as she reached for him. When Mirrin scratched his head, he purred and leaned into her hand.

"Yes. He became what I needed, and I needed someone to care for who would offer me comfort. I take care of him; he takes care of me."

"I am glad that you have each other. You wrote that you met your twin?"

"I did. Luken is inside."

"He is a sweet boy, but you are on different paths. Don't forget that. He cannot go where you do, but you will always be twins."

Imara sighed and turned, hugging her mother tightly. "I know. I know where my path is leading, and Redbird City fits into my plans."

When Imara straightened, she wiped the tears from her eyes. "So, did you want to come into the party? If you have never seen an elf and a specter cut a rug, now is your chance."

Mirrin laughed. "I can't resist an invitation like that. Please, introduce me to your friends."

Mr. E sat up straight as if trying to make a good impression, and Imara led her mother into her party.

It was a great end to her first term, even if most of the party was more dead than alive; they were her chosen company.

Mirrin watched Liirick trying to teach Imara to swing dance while her familiar consumed the cake.

"So, Reegar, do you regret taking her

in?"

"Ah, dearest Chancellor, I don't regret it for a moment. She understands the needs of the dead more than we even do. She has crafted a trust fund for me for a few years after she leaves, so that I will never be without the ability to become physical in my own home. How thoughtful is that?"

Mirrin eyed her youngest son and the woman he was flirting with. "What about her?"

"Bara is a legacy to my hall. She enjoys the library and that is all that I need to know most days. The addition of your son is causing a bit of a stir, but she is nearing graduation and will need to choose her path. If she wants to further her education, I am still here."

"What about next term? Will you take in more students?"

"I will take two more in. I am going to choose carefully."

"Good. Perhaps we can arrange to change your façade as well."

Reegar smiled. "It is a thought. I will bear it in mind. I am beginning to like hosting students."

"It only took eighty years. Not bad."

"Mirrin."

"Yes?"

"Thank you for coming. I wasn't sure you would when I sent the invitation."

"Thank you for inviting me. She didn't mention it in our last letter."

"She didn't know. This was our party for her. She has made an impression on those around her, and this is her reward. If the reward has to come from the dead, so be it."

"She is that powerful?"

"Getting stronger every day, and I am happy to be here to see it. She hasn't given me life again, but she has let me come to grips with what I was missing by not engaging with the world I am still present in."

"That is quite the gift."

"And she gives it without knowing. So, be proud of your daughter and send her a card in that enchanted box of yours. If her brothers are anything like her, you should be very proud."

Mirrin chuckled. "I will. I knew the moment I held her that she was going to make a mark in the world, and I just hoped that she would be happy doing it. Today was a huge leap for her, and I am delighted that you are there to catch her on the other side."

There was a lot of meaning in those words as they hung in the air between them.

As Imara's enjoyment expanded, the ghosts got stronger, and soon, the entire spectral population of the college was bopping and twirling. Mirrin watched her daughter's effect and wondered at the luck that had brought them together again.

Then again, with a seventh of seven involved, luck was always a factor.

So, we have seen the first book of five that will take Imara through her college days and out into the world.

The Hellkitten Chronicles will cross with the "An Obscure Magic" universe, though it will be exclusively Imara's story with Mr. E by her side.

Now, as for Mr. E. He is based on my own fur baby, born August 30th with dark chocolate, charcoal and black-striped fur. Only the tip of his tail is white, and his orange eyes are wide and soulful. He is also a goof, eats anything I do before I can and turns up where he shouldn't, a living shadow. The fictional kitten will eventually grow up but not until Imara graduates.

The next book in this series is *Shape Shifting 201*.

Thanks for reading,

Viola Grace

About the Author

Viola Grace (aka Zenina Masters) is a Canadian sci-fi/paranormal romance writer with ambitions to keep writing for the rest of her life. She specializes in short stories because the thrill of discovery, of all those firsts, is what keeps her writing.

An artist who enjoys a story that catches you up, whirls you around and sets you down with a smile on your face is all she endeavours to be. She prefers to leave the drama to those who are better suited to it, she always goes for the cheap laugh.

www.ingramcontent.com/pod-product-compliance
Lightning Source LLC
Chambersburg PA
CBHW071928190726
48293CB00004B/1202